A Gift
of the
Sands

STACEY INTERNATIONAL

London

A GIFT OF THE SANDS

published by

Stacey International

128 Kensington Church Street

London W8 4BH

Tel: 020 7221 7166 Fax: 020 7792 9288

E-mail: enquiries@stacey-international.co.uk

Website: www.stacey-international.co.uk

ISBN: 1 900988 917

CIP Data: A catalogue record for this book is available from the British Library

© Julia Johnson and Emily Styles 2005

1 3 5 7 9 0 8 6 4 2

Design: Kitty Carruthers

Printing & Binding: SNP Leefung, China

A Gift
of the
Sands

Story
Julia Johnson

Illustrations
Emily Styles

For
Alice and William

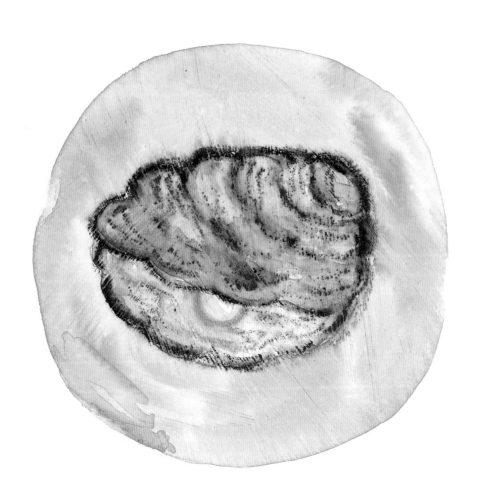

Long ago in the warm waters of the Arabian Gulf there lived an oyster. A grain of sand tickled him and so he made a pearl round it. After many years the pearl had grown very big and very beautiful. "I must be the finest pearl in the whole world," it thought proudly.

One day the oyster was
washed into a rock pool
by the tide. A gull saw the
oyster as it dived low over
the pools looking for
something to eat. The bird
picked up the oyster and dropped
it onto the rocks to break open the
shell. "Now I shall be found," thought
the pearl, "and everyone will gasp when
they see how beautiful I am."

But the bird was too busy gobbling up the oyster to notice the pearl fall out of the shell. As it rolled over the rocks it tried to stop, but it was so round and shiny it just gathered speed. Suddenly it found itself falling back into the blue waters of the ocean. "No! No!" cried the pearl. "Who's going to find me here?"

Well, it did not have long to wait. As the pearl dropped through the water, a red snapper swam by and swallowed it up. "Goodness me! How rude! Doesn't this fish realize who I am?" the pearl muttered to itself, and it bounced up and down crossly. "I am the finest pearl in the world and I'm not staying here, that's for sure," and it wriggled and jiggled around angrily in the fish's stomach.

The red snapper soon began to feel a nasty pain. The pearl was making him feel very uncomfortable and he didn't look where he was going. He swam right into the fisherman's net.

When his net was full the fisherman called to his friends to help him drag it ashore.

"Something's happening," thought the pearl. "Soon I shall be found. Then I shall be given to a Sultan, and when he sees how magnificent I am he'll surround me with rubies and diamonds and wear me on his finger." And the pearl wriggled and jiggled about impatiently.

Before long traders joined the fisherman on the beach and bought the catch. Then the pearl found itself going on a bumpy ride. The fish were being taken to market. All day long people came to the market to buy the fish, and the pearl could hear voices bargaining for a good price. It wriggled and jiggled about hopefully, expecting the fish in which it was hidden to be sold at any moment.

But at the end of the day no one had bought the red snapper. The fish was no longer fresh, so the stall-holder threw it to a hungry cat that was looking for some supper.

The cat ran off with his prize and found a quiet corner, where he tucked into the fish contentedly. "Daylight at last," thought the pearl, as it rolled away. Suddenly it was engulfed by a huge wave of water – a man with a hose was cleaning the market place – and the pearl was carried off towards the gutter. "No! No! Stop!" cried the pearl. "Don't you know who I am?"

A little boy was having fun jumping over the water as it swept towards the drain. The pearl caught his eye, and he reached down and snatched it up just in time. "Now I shall be taken to the Sultan," thought the pearl, and it wriggled and jiggled about excitedly in the little boy's pocket.

The little boy climbed into a truck beside his father and they set off for home. It was a long drive out of town to the green oasis where the boy lived with his family.

By the time they reached the village the little boy was asleep. His mother gently lifted him down from the truck. Without waking him she laid him down on his sleeping mat.

In the morning the little boy put on a clean *dishdasha* and set out for school. He forgot all about the pearl.

His mother collected the dirty clothes and tied them up in a cloth. The pearl found itself far too close to some smelly socks. "Good gracious me! This is no way to treat the finest pearl in the world!" and it wriggled and jiggled about indignantly in the pocket.

The woman gathered up the bundle and took the clothes to the pool to wash. The pearl was slapped against a rock as the woman scrubbed the *dishdasha* clean. "Ouch!" it yelled furiously, but the woman did not hear. Soon she picked up the wet clothes and took them home.

As she shook out the *dishdasha* the pearl found itself flying through the air once more. "Now where am I off to?" it demanded angrily. It fell into the grass and was hidden from view.

Some time later a busy hoopoe was digging for insects with its long beak. "Watch it!" shrieked the pearl. "Don't prod me! Don't you know that I am the finest pearl in the world?" "*Hud hud*!" cried the hoopoe. "Look what I have found!"

A mynah bird heard the hoopoe's message and flew down from his perch in the date palm tree. "Now there's a pretty thing!" it squawked, and it hopped up and down delightedly. Very carefully it picked up the pearl in its beak and flew off with it towards its nest. "I hope this bird knows the way to the palace," thought the pearl hopefully. It wriggled and jiggled about impatiently.

The mynah tried its best to hold onto the pearl, but as it flew over a patch of alfalfa the pearl slipped from its beak and disappeared amongst the waving stalks. The mynah searched for it for a little while, but when it could not find the pearl it lost interest and flew off to look for another treasure.

"No one will find me here," thought the pearl sadly.

But it was wrong!

Before long a farmer came by with a long knife and cut down the alfalfa. He piled it up high and tied some string around it. The pearl found itself right in the middle of the bundle. Before it knew what was happening it was being strapped to the side of a camel. "We must be going on a journey," it thought excitedly, "a journey to the palace." And it wriggled and jiggled about happily.

The camel set off. Soon they were out in the desert far away from the oasis. The pearl wanted to see where it was going but it was squeezed too tightly between the alfalfa stalks. It swayed from side to side as the camel's rolling gait carried it onwards.

After several hours the camel caravan came to a
halt. The pearl could hear men's voices shouting.
The camels were unloaded and the alfalfa was
untied and spread out before the them. "Oh no!"
shouted the pearl in horror, and it rolled out of the
way just as a big open mouth reached down
towards it.

The pearl lay in the hot sand long after the camels had gone on their way. What was to become of it now? No one would find it here. There was nothing but sand as far as the eye could see.

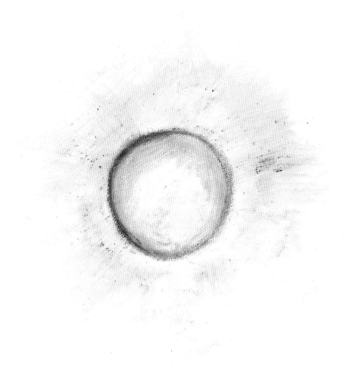

But it was wrong!

From out of nowhere a jerboa appeared!
Sheltering from the heat at the
entrance to its burrow it had
seen the pearl shimmer
in the sunlight.

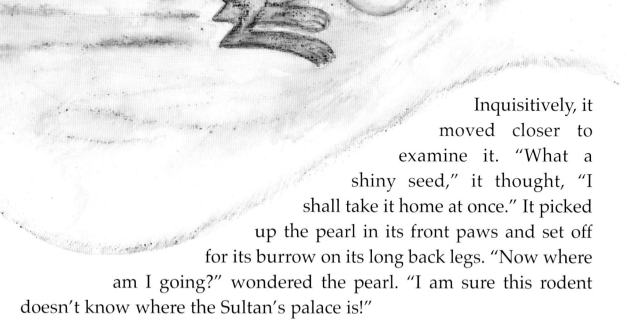

Inquisitively, it
moved closer to
examine it. "What a
shiny seed," it thought, "I
shall take it home at once." It picked
up the pearl in its front paws and set off
for its burrow on its long back legs. "Now where
am I going?" wondered the pearl. "I am sure this rodent
doesn't know where the Sultan's palace is!"

And it was right!

When the jerboa reached its burrow it stopped. "I'll just have a little bite to make sure this seed is tasty for my children," said the jerboa.

"Oh no you don't!" shouted the pearl and it w^{riggled} ^{and} $_{jiggled}$ frantically, "Why does everybody want to eat me? Can't you see that I'm the finest pearl in the world? Don't you dare spoil my beautiful shiny skin!"

Too late! The jerboa gnawed with its long front teeth, but drew back when it discovered how hard the pearl was.

"Serves you right! Hope you break your teeth," muttered the pearl indignantly. The jerboa dropped it and scuttled off down its hole.

So there was the pearl alone once more. It lay there looking up at the bright hot sun in the vastness of the blue sky. All around, the desert stretched away – there were more grains of sand than anyone could ever count in a whole lifetime.

Suddenly, the pearl felt very, very small. "Perhaps I'm not the finest pearl in the world after all." And it thought about all the things which had happened to it.

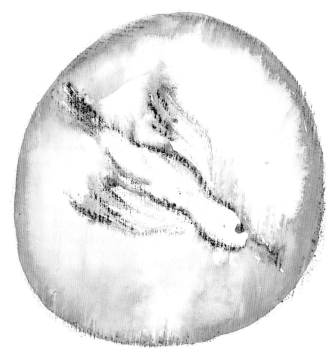

The pearl remembered the moment it had first seen daylight when the gull broke the oyster shell open. How eager it had been to be taken to the Sultan!

It remembered
how it had been
swallowed by
the red snapper,
how the little boy
had saved it from
the drain, and
how it had
been lost again
in the grass where a
hoopoe had found it.

Then it had been carried through the air in the mynah bird's beak, but dropped in the patch of alfalfa.

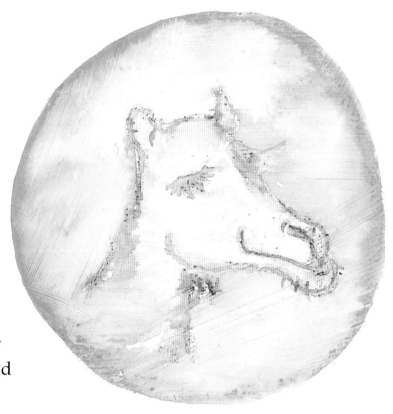

When the alfalfa had been fed to the camels, the pearl had narrowly escaped being eaten! A jerboa had tried to eat it too! No one had cared about the pearl's worth. And it remembered how angry and impatient it had been.

Then another thought came to it. "I must have had more adventures than most pearls ever dream about. Maybe I'm the luckiest pearl in the world." It began to wonder about this, and the pearl thought it might have enjoyed its adventures more if it had not been so anxious to be taken to the Sultan all the time. "Perhaps I am never going to see a palace," the pearl thought.

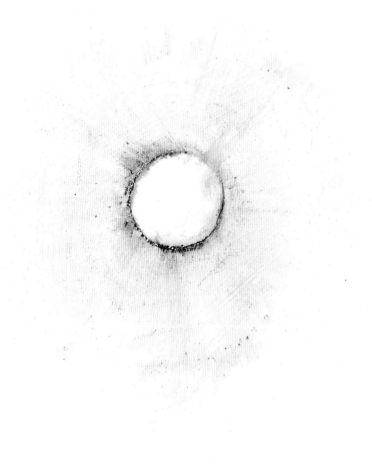

For many days the pearl lay in the desert and it had time to look around. It stopped worrying about what was to become of it. Instead it became one with the sand and the sun and the sky. It was thankful for the softness of the sand in which it was lying. It was grateful for the beauty of the desert stretching away to the far horizon, and it stared in wonder at the vast canopy of the blue sky overhead. It was comforted when the sun stroked it with its beams and made it glimmer, and it loved the night enfolding it in its blanket of darkness.

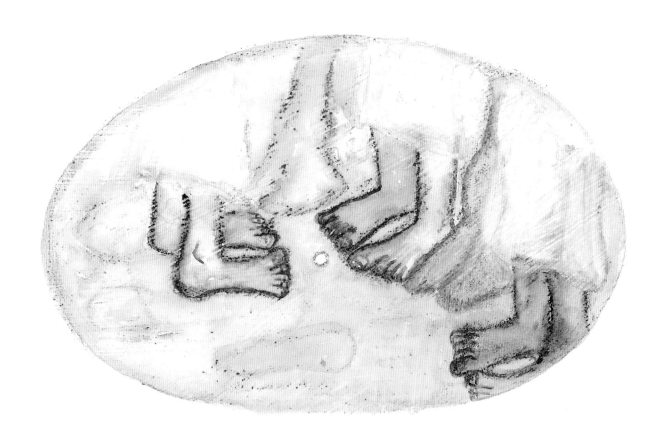

And so it was with surprise that the pearl heard the camel caravan returning. Soon it was surrounded by camels and men. The men took off their *agals,* the coiled braid which held their *shemaghs* in place on their heads. Then they hobbled the camels with the *agals* to prevent them straying far away. Some of camels were encouraged to sit and provide shade for the men.

Twigs were gathered, and soon a small fire was
burning and the men made coffee. They ate dates and
sipped their coffee and shared conversation.

Darkness
fell, and the
men smoked and
drank more coffee and
talked into the night.
Their journey had been
long and they were
happy to rest a while.

A young man was sitting very close to the pearl and the pearl could hear what he was saying. It seemed that the young man wished to marry a beautiful girl from a neighbouring tribe, but the girl's father refused to consider the young man for his daughter. He simply wasn't rich enough! The young man looked sad, and the pearl felt sorry for him.

Then the pearl had an idea. Perhaps it was a very fine pearl, perhaps it was even the finest pearl in the world! Perhaps it was just not meant for the Sultan. But perhaps ... it was meant for this young man! The pearl wriggled and jiggled excitedly.

Suddenly a silver finger of moonlight stroked the
pearl and it glimmered and shimmered more brightly
than it had ever done before. At that moment the
young man turned. He stared at the pearl as if he
couldn't believe his eyes. With trembling fingers he
picked it up. The others gathered round to look. They
passed the pearl from one to another.

"This is a gift from Allah, you are rich my son," an old man declared. "Do you think it's really meant for me?" the young man asked. "Of course. Allah saw your sadness. Now you can be happy and marry the girl you love." And the others agreed. "Take it," they said, "we shall rejoice in your happiness."

And so it was that the pearl found itself hanging from a fine gold chain around the neck of the beautiful young girl on her wedding day.

"This must be the finest pearl in the world," the girl said to the young man, "for without it I would not have you." And the young man's heart was filled with joy.

The old man had finished his story. The little boy looked up. "Is it true, grandfather?" he asked.

The old man smiled, "Haven't you noticed the beautiful pearl which your mother always wears?" The little boy nodded. "It was found in the desert, a gift in the sand, but no one truly knows how it got there," the old man told him.

"And is it the finest pearl in the world, grandfather?" the little boy asked.

"Who can say?" the old man replied, "The seas have many oysters. But one thing is certain, to your mother and father it is certainly the finest pearl in the world!"

Glossary

agal	the coilded black braid used to hold the headcloth in place. It was also used for hobbling a camel's front legs so that it did not stray too far
alfalfa	a crop grown to feed camels
camel caravan	a group of people and their camels travelling together for security
dishdasha	a long, white, loose-fitting garment worn by men and boys
hoopoe	a pretty bird with black and white bars on its wings, a crest of feathers on its head, and a long, curved beak. It spends a lot of time on the ground jabbing for insects
hud hud	the Arabic name for the hoopoe, and the sound of its distinctive cry
jerboa	a desert rodent, with small front legs and strong back ones for jumping, and a long tail which it uses for balancing
oasis	a green area in the desert, where people settle because water is found there
red snapper	a fish with a dark pink shine to its scales
shemagh	a red and white checked headcloth worn by men and boys
Sultan	an important nobleman, similar to a king